W9-BDV-042

When Chickens Grow Teeth

A Story from the French of · GUY DE MAUPASSANT ·

Retold and Illustrated by

WENDY · ANDERSON · HALPERIN

ORCHARD BOOKS · NEW YORK

Orchard Books • 95 Madison Avenue • New York, NY 10016

Manufactured in the United States of America. Printed by Barton Press, Inc. Bound by Horowitz/Rae. Book design by Jean Krulis. The text of this book is set in 14 point Weiss. The illustrations are pencil and watercolor reproduced in full color.

1 3 5 7 9 10 8 6 4 2

Library of Congress Cataloging-in-Publication Data
Halperin, Wendy Anderson. "When chickens grow teeth" : a story from the French of Guy de Maupassant / retold and illustrated by Wendy Anderson Halperin. p. cm. "A Richard Jackson book"—Half t.p. Summary: A cafe keeper in a small French village cannot escape from his wife's silly plan to have him hatch eggs in the bed to which he is confined. ISBN 0-531-09526-6. — ISBN 0-531-08876-6 (lib. bdg.) [1. Chickens—Fiction. 2. Eggs—Fiction.] I. Maupassant, Guy de, 1850–1893. II. Title.
PZ7.H16555Wh 1996 [E]—dc20 95-53797

To Richard Jackson and his way with words,

to Phil and people like him who care about the living conditions of chickens,

to Gérard Depardieu and the creators of French films,

to the Chicago Public Library (a great place to do research), and

to my parents, my friends, Haas and Andy

In a small French village as old as the stones, there lives a large, laughing man named Antoine. He is the café keeper and he is large because, for every cream puff he sells, he eats a second. For every glassful of lemonade he pours, he takes another glassful himself.

The man has no children of his own, but he calls friend and follower alike "old son." They, in turn, call him Toine and come every day to his Café des Amis for a delicious pastry, or a game of dominoes or bocci ball, or simply for the pleasure of the man's good company.

Toine gets
along happily with everyone . . .
except his wife, Madame Colette.

You see,
Madame Colette has
the temper of a wild boar.

She raises chickens behind the café. With her pointed nose, stiltlike legs, and cackling tongue, she seems like a chicken herself. Her head bobs back and forth on her outstretched neck.

"You lazy oaf," she snaps, seeing Toine with two friends at chess. "Stop your gabbing and laughing and stuffing your belly, and be of some help to me, eh?" To the others she complains, "A big tub of lard like that should be in a sty with the pigs!"

People come from all over to buy her eggs, just as they come from all over to visit Toine. But they do not count on her for good company. No, no, no, it's in the coop that you'll find Madame Colette.

One day
Toine is hanging
fresh cheese on a hook when the cat jumps and startles him. With a shout of surprise Toine topples off the ladder and lands with a *thud*!

The great good-hearted man cannot get up. It takes six of his friends to carry him to his bed next door.

"Ah, but I'm aching all over," he groans. "I need some bread, old sons, and a cream puff. Then I'll be up and about again."

At the window the red rooster who likes Toine's company (and also bread crumbs) crows and crows, telling all the countryside of Toine's fall.

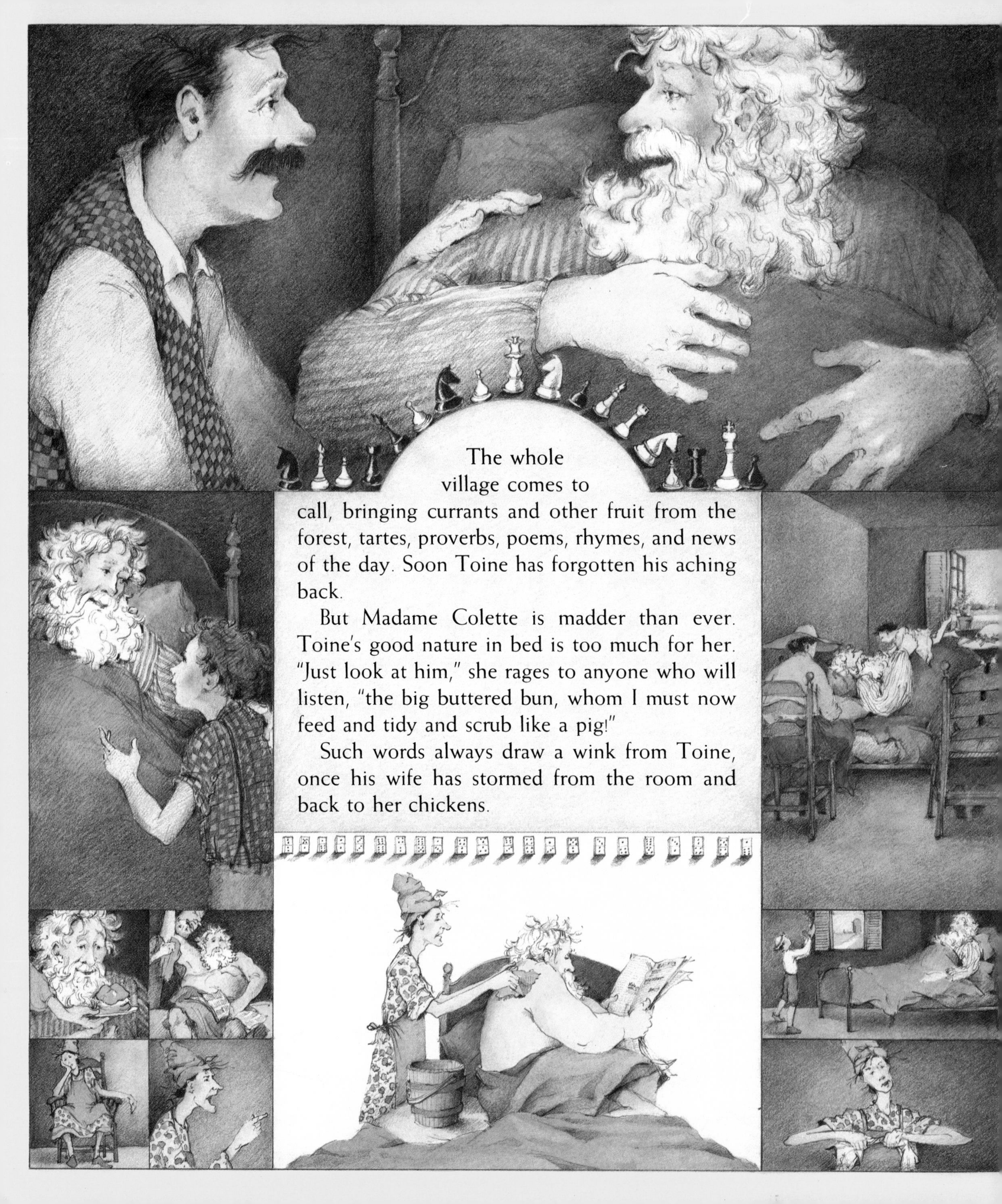

The whole
village comes to
call, bringing currants and other fruit from the forest, tartes, proverbs, poems, rhymes, and news of the day. Soon Toine has forgotten his aching back.

But Madame Colette is madder than ever. Toine's good nature in bed is too much for her. "Just look at him," she rages to anyone who will listen, "the big buttered bun, whom I must now feed and tidy and scrub like a pig!"

Such words always draw a wink from Toine, once his wife has stormed from the room and back to her chickens.

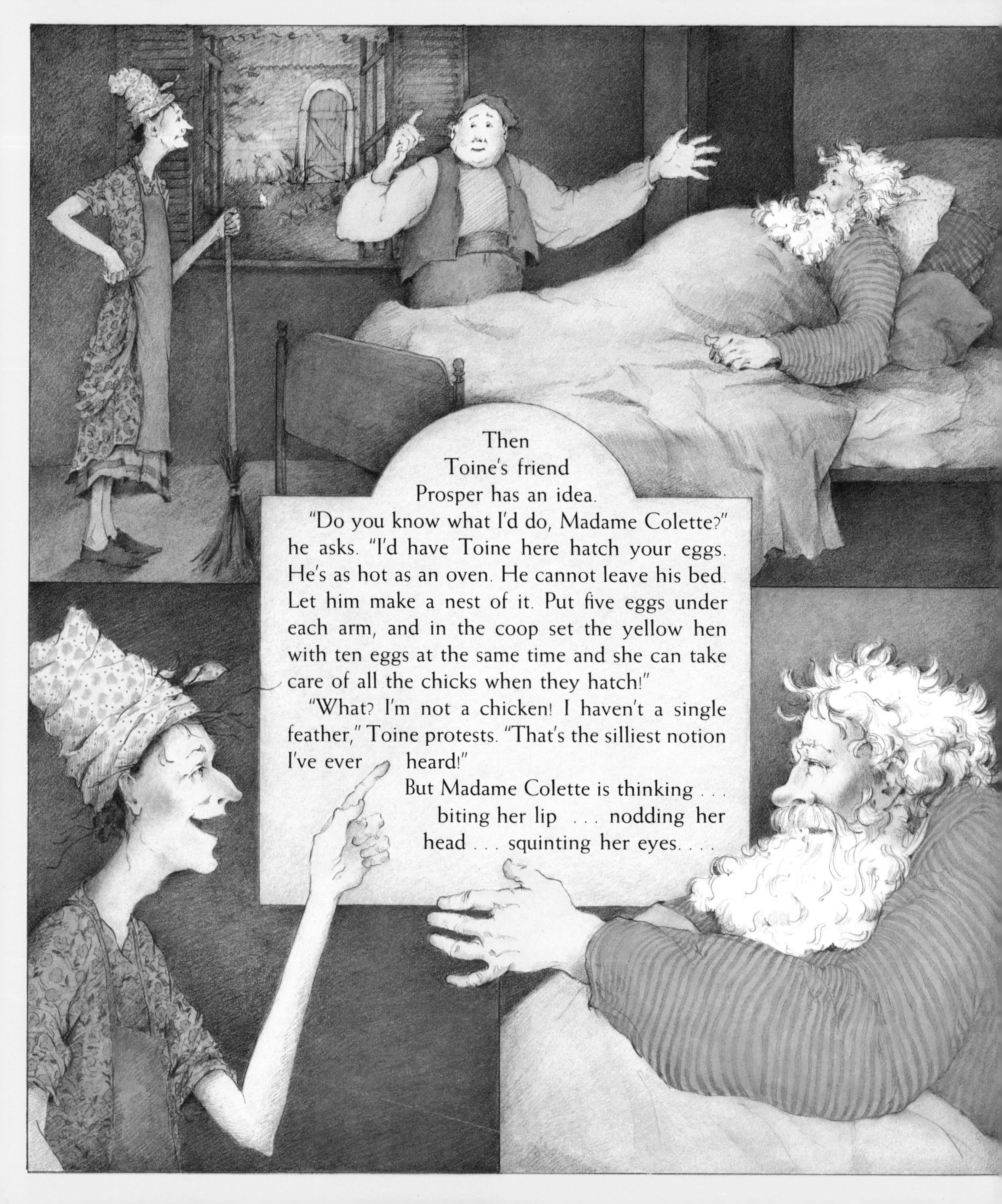

Then
Toine's friend
Prosper has an idea.

"Do you know what I'd do, Madame Colette?" he asks. "I'd have Toine here hatch your eggs. He's as hot as an oven. He cannot leave his bed. Let him make a nest of it. Put five eggs under each arm, and in the coop set the yellow hen with ten eggs at the same time and she can take care of all the chicks when they hatch!"

"What? I'm not a chicken! I haven't a single feather," Toine protests. "That's the silliest notion I've ever heard!"

But Madame Colette is thinking . . . biting her lip . . . nodding her head . . . squinting her eyes. . . .

"*Ooo la la la la* . . . I'll hatch eggs when chickens grow teeth."

CAFE DES AMIS

The next
morning Madame Colette
tells her chickens, "I have news, my lovelies. The great oaf will be helping to hatch your eggs!"

Clucking, she returns to Toine. "I have just put the yellow hen to set with ten eggs under her. Here are yours. Be careful, you good-for-nothing, not to break them!"

Toine is astonished by the ten eggs in her apron. "You cannot mean this, woman!" he cries. "Now take those eggs and make your poor husband an omelette for breakfast."

"No breakfast for you, you overstuffed cream puff. Or dinner either until you tend to your duty. You and the yellow hen, you are both on your nests now, ha-ha!"

You can imagine what Toine's visitors think, just when he is beginning to look ready to rise from bed without groaning.

But knowing Madame Colette's vile temper, they commence to bring him pillows.

With a sigh (for he is faint with hunger now), Toine fluffs up his nest, rolls five eggs under each elbow, and settles his great arms gently. Relenting, Madame Colette bobs her head and brings him a big pot of soup and fresh bread.

Soon the room is filled with roars of belly laughter and merriment, until Toine, unable to resist an audience, tries to make an egg disappear by magic and rolls one—*crack!*—onto the floor.

Oh, the shrieking then as Madame Colette comes running! "Every egg you break," she cries, "means a whole day for you without a bite to eat."

Poor Toine. What choice does he have?

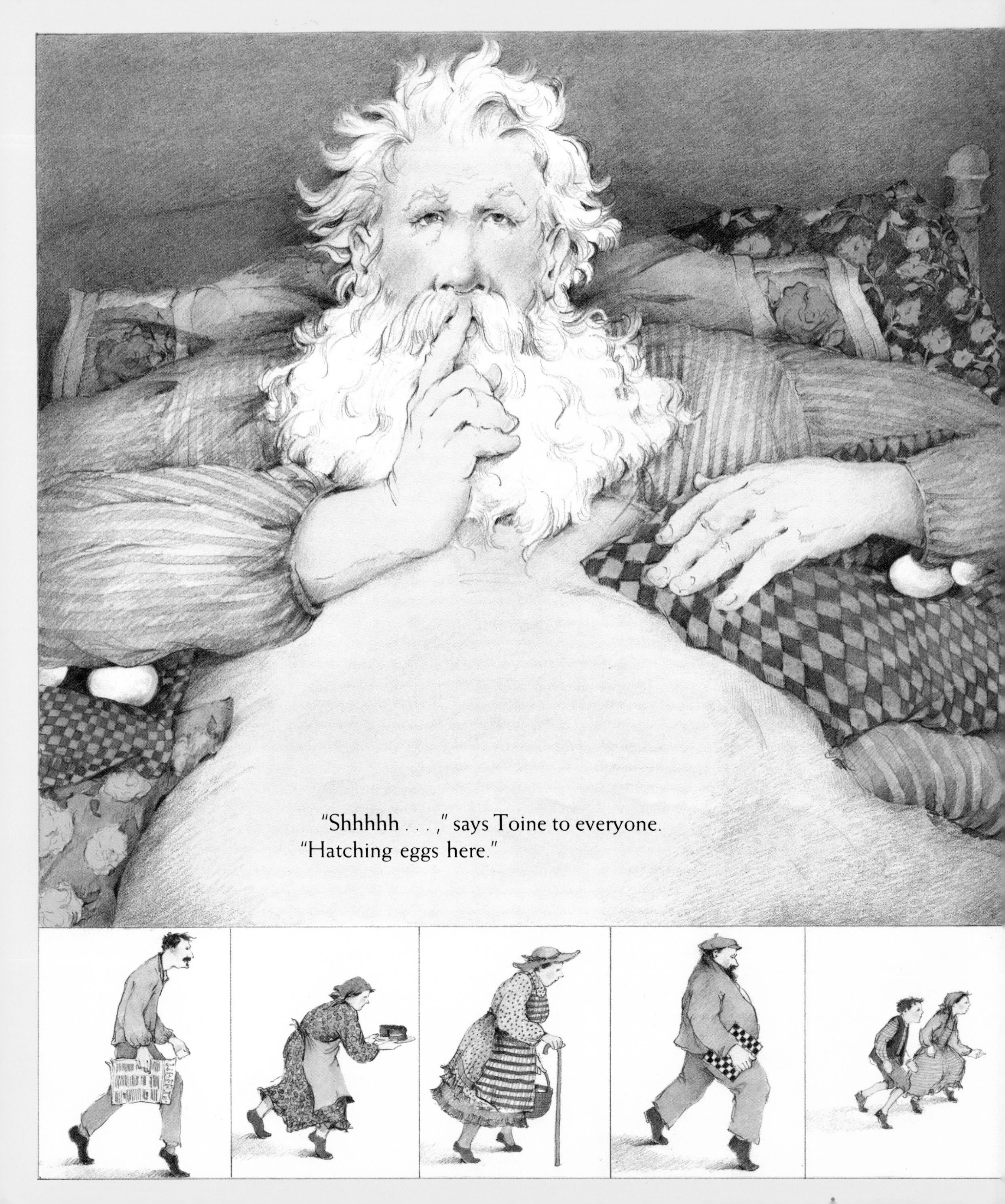

"Shhhhh . . . ," says Toine to everyone. "Hatching eggs here."

Time slows.
And soon the rollicking Toine is becoming "broody." Like the hen in the chicken coop he protects those nine remaining eggs with his life. And for his trouble he is eating regularly. Once, even, a cream puff.

His friends still come, but on tiptoe now.

"Don't bump the bed," Toine whispers. "And keep your voices down. Play softly, old son," he tells Jean, his friend with the accordion. "Some music for my lovely eggs."

You know, don't you, that an egg takes twenty-one days to hatch?

And all
the twenty-one
long days, Madame Colette struts from hen to husband and husband to hen.

Finally she announces, "The yellow hen has hatched an egg!" Later, another . . . and another . . . and another until by day's end there are seven new chicks in the poultry yard. "Three eggs," Madame Colette admits, "were bad."

Old Toine's heart beats fast and faster to think of it. He wonders how many chicks he'll have, what they will look like, and if any will love cream puffs like their father.

That is how Toine is thinking of himself. For days he has been saving bread crumbs for his chicks' first meal.

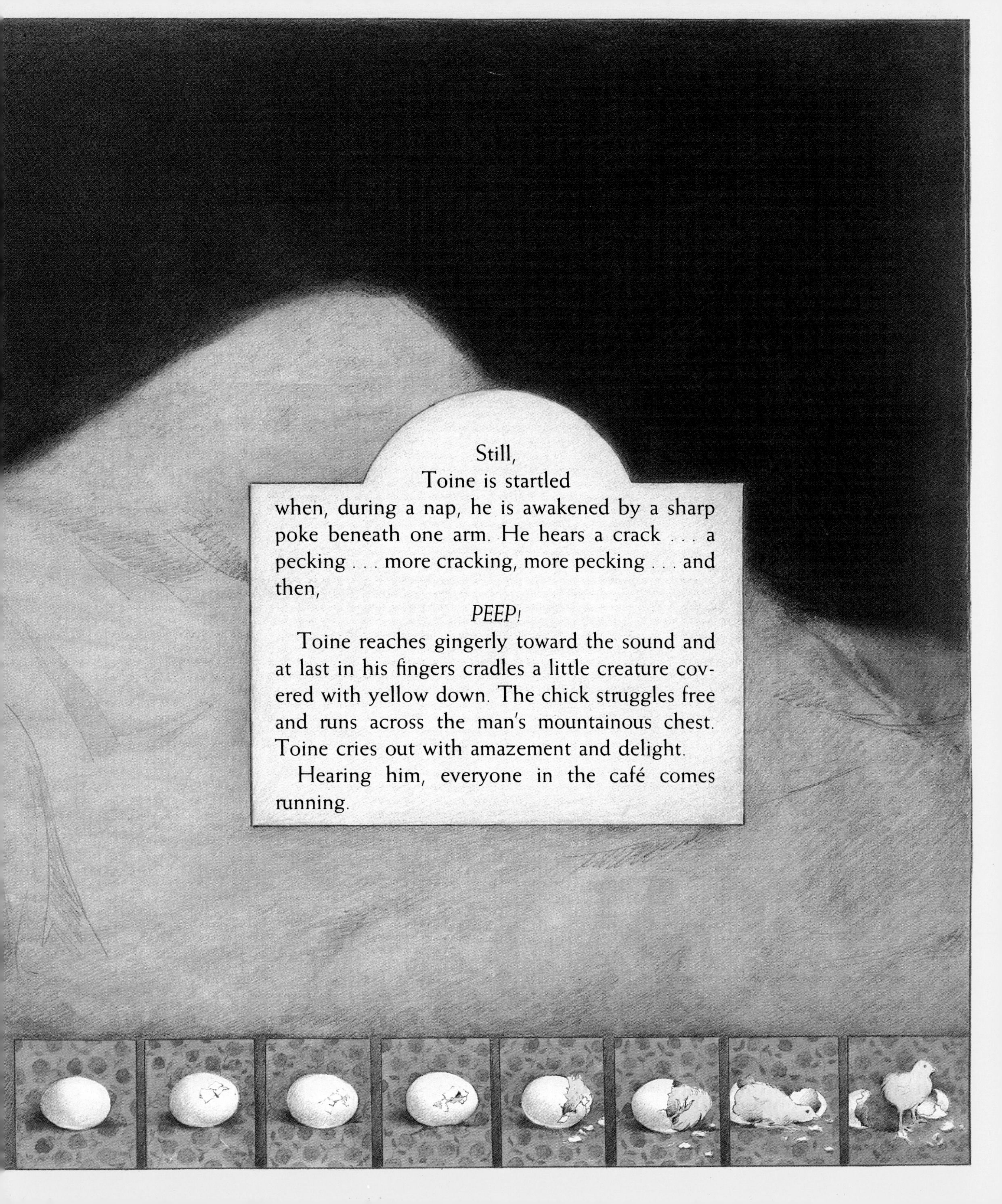

Still,
Toine is startled
when, during a nap, he is awakened by a sharp poke beneath one arm. He hears a crack . . . a pecking . . . more cracking, more pecking . . . and then,

PEEP!

Toine reaches gingerly toward the sound and at last in his fingers cradles a little creature covered with yellow down. The chick struggles free and runs across the man's mountainous chest. Toine cries out with amazement and delight.

Hearing him, everyone in the café comes running.

"Old father Toine, you did it!"

"Bravo! Congratulations!"

"*Sacre bleu*. Looks like you, Toine. Wonderfully round!"

"Can I see it?"

"Can I hold it?"

"*Ooo la la*. Truly it's a miracle."

Just then Toine cries, "Here comes another one, by heavens!"

They all listen to the sounds of cracking and pecking . . . and then to a *PEEP*! This chick nestles in Toine's soft beard. "Madame Colette, come and see!"

His wife
scurries in, a
smile breaking out despite herself.

"By heavens, here come some more," Toine bellows.

All afternoon . . . cracking and pecking and *peep, peep, peep, peep, peep, peep.*

There are eggshells everywhere on the bed, cries of happiness on every mouth.

At sunset Madame Colette proudly places eight baby chicks under the yellow hen in the poultry yard.

But under Toine's left arm there is a ninth egg, still unhatched. And so it stays, silent, until the moon rises and poor old Toine, an exhausted parent, falls asleep.

Sometime
in the dark of the
night, Toine feels a *poke* under his arm.

The last chick is arriving! The crackings and peckings sound like claps in the quiet darkness. The chick *PEEPS* at last, but not so loud that Madame Colette wakes.

Toine smiles kindly at the baby. "I hope you like it here, my sweet feathered friend. I have bread crumbs for you, and a little water. Perhaps you will even like cream puffs, too, eh? We all have been waiting and hoping for you. . . . See? There is the moon smiling down."

Toine's joy fills him fuller than any feast.

In the
morning Madame Colette
holds her hand out for the chick. But Toine asks, as a young boy might, "May I keep this one? I am strong enough to be out of bed. This little chick has taken up my aches and pains."

"Keep it, husband? Why, that's the silliest idea I've ever heard," Madame Colette declares, and carries the chick away.

How Toine misses his babies' peeping and cheeping. Are they eating well? he worries, even during a chess game. Are they warm enough? Do they think of me?

That night, for no reason Toine guesses, the red rooster crows at his window. My chicks, Toine thinks in a panic. In his sail-sized nightshirt he hobbles to the coop.

Oh, but the chicks are fine, fine!

To this
day you will find
old father Toine tending those beloved chickens as proudly as any parent. Not one has shown a taste for cream puffs—but Toine only laughs, and says, "The more for me, eh, old son?"

Even Madame Colette is happier now. Perhaps because Toine is now part of the flock.

He lets the chickens roost in trees. That's what they prefer, you know. Even Madame Colette helps the little ones up.

And have those chickens grown teeth? Perhaps! Stranger and more wonderful things have happened.

Ooo la la la la.